W6-BAU-360

A Note to Parents and Caregivers:

Read-it! Readers are for children who are just starting on the amazing road to reading. These beautiful books support both the acquisition of reading skills and the love of books.

 The PURPLE LEVEL presents basic topics and objects using high frequency words and simple language patterns.

 The RED LEVEL presents familiar topics using common words and repeating sentence patterns.

 The BLUE LEVEL presents new ideas using a larger vocabulary and varied sentence structure.

 The YELLOW LEVEL presents more challenging ideas, a broad vocabulary, and wide variety in sentence structure.

 The GREEN LEVEL presents more complex ideas, an extended vocabulary range, and expanded language structures.

 The ORANGE LEVEL presents a wide range of ideas and concepts using challenging vocabulary and complex language structures.

When sharing a book with your child, read in short stretches, pausing often to talk about the pictures. Have your child turn the pages and point to the pictures and familiar words. And be sure to reread favorite stories or parts of stories.

There is no right or wrong way to share books with children. Find time to read with your child, and pass on the legacy of literacy.

Adria F. Klein, Ph.D.
Professor Emeritus
California State University
San Bernardino, California

Editor: Christianne Jones
Designer: Amy Muehlenhardt
Page Production: Michelle Biedscheid
Art Director: Nathan Gassman
The illustrations in this book were created in watercolor and pencil.

Picture Window Books
5115 Excelsior Boulevard
Suite 232
Minneapolis, MN 55416
877-845-8392
www.picturewindowbooks.com

Copyright © 2008 by Picture Window Books
All rights reserved. No part of this book may be reproduced without written
permission from the publisher. The publisher takes no responsibility for the use of
any of the materials or methods described in this book, nor for the products thereof.

Printed in the United States of America.

All books published by Picture Window Books
are manufactured with paper containing at least
10 percent post-consumer waste.

Library of Congress Cataloging-in-Publication Data
Klein, Adria F. (Adria Fay), 1947-
Max goes to the playground / by Adria F. Klein ; illustrated by Mernie
Gallagher-Cole.
p. cm. — (Read-it! readers. The life of Max)
Summary: While at the playground, Max and his friend José swing, climb, and slide
all day long.
ISBN-13: 978-1-4048-3681-5 (library binding)
ISBN-10: 1-4048-3681-0 (library binding)
[1. Playgrounds—Fiction. 2. Play—Fiction. 3. Friendship—Fiction.] I. Gallagher-
Cole, Mernie, ill. II. Title.
PZ7.K678324Maxp 2007
[E]—dc22   2007004056

Max
Goes to the
Playground

by Adria F. Klein
illustrated by Mernie Gallagher-Cole

Special thanks to our advisers for their expertise:

Adria F. Klein, Ph.D.
Professor Emeritus, California State University
San Bernardino, California

Susan Kesselring, M.A., Literacy Educator
Rosemount–Apple Valley–Eagan (Minnesota) School District

PiCTURE WiNDOW BOOKS
Minneapolis, Minnesota

Max is going to the playground.

He invites his friend José.

Max and José play on the jungle gym.

They race to the top.

Max plays on the merry-go-round.

He spins so fast his hat blows off!

José plays on the slide.

He slides down ten times.

Max and José play on the orange seesaw. They go up and down as fast as they can.

Then they try to balance in the middle.

Max and José play on the swings.

They take turns pushing each other.

Max climbs up the cargo net.

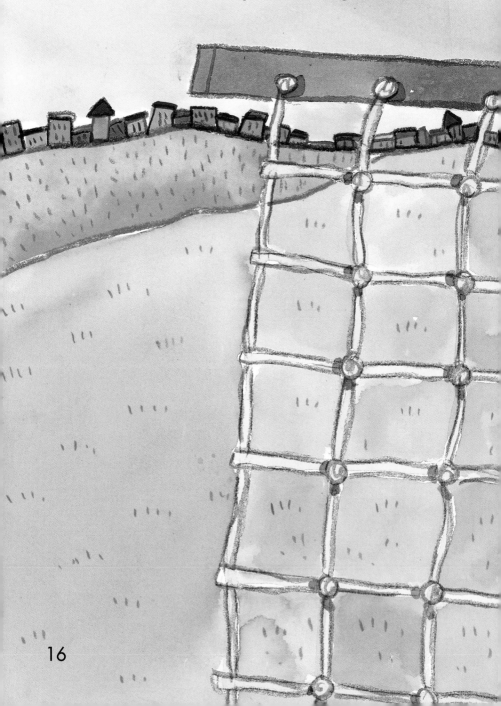

Oh, no! His shoe gets stuck!

José slides down the fireman's pole to help.

19

Max and José are tired.

They lie down and watch the clouds.

Max and José walk home. They had a lot of fun at the playground.

More *Read-it!* Readers

Bright pictures and fun stories help you practice your reading skills. Look for more books at your level.

Max Goes on the Bus	*Max and Buddy Go to the Vet*
Max Goes Shopping	*Max and the Adoption Day Party*
Max Goes to School	*Max Celebrates Chinese New Year*
Max Goes to the Barber	*Max Goes to a Cookout*
Max Goes to the Dentist	*Max Goes to the Farm*
Max Goes to the Doctor	*Max Goes to the Grocery Store*
Max Goes to the Library	*Max Learns Sign Language*
Max Goes to the Zoo	*Max Stays Overnight*
	Max's Fun Day

On the Web

FactHound offers a safe, fun way to find Web sites related to this book. All of the sites on FactHound have been researched by our staff.

1. Visit *www.facthound.com*
2. Type in this special code: 1404836810
3. Click on the FETCH IT button.

Your trusty FactHound will fetch the best sites for you!
A complete list of *Read-it!* Readers is available on our Web site:
www.picturewindowbooks.com

No longer property of the
Dayton Metro Library

WC

0006091875085

9-24-08

Dayton Metro Library

Max goes to the playground /

KLEIN
Klein, Adria F. 1947-
Pb   KLEIN